Ravena

Ravena

Olivier Dunrea

Holiday House/New York

Copyright © 1984 by Olivier Dunrea
All rights reserved
Printed in the United States of America
First Edition

Library of Congress
Cataloging in Publication Data

Dunrea, Olivier.
Ravena.

Summary: Miserable Ravena, a banshee who
doesn't fit in, leaves home in search of
someplace that will suit her better.
[1. Fairies—Fiction] I. Title.
PZ7.D922Rav 1984   [E]   82-23244
ISBN 0-8234-0487-0

Ravena is, and always will be,
for Margery and Wayne!

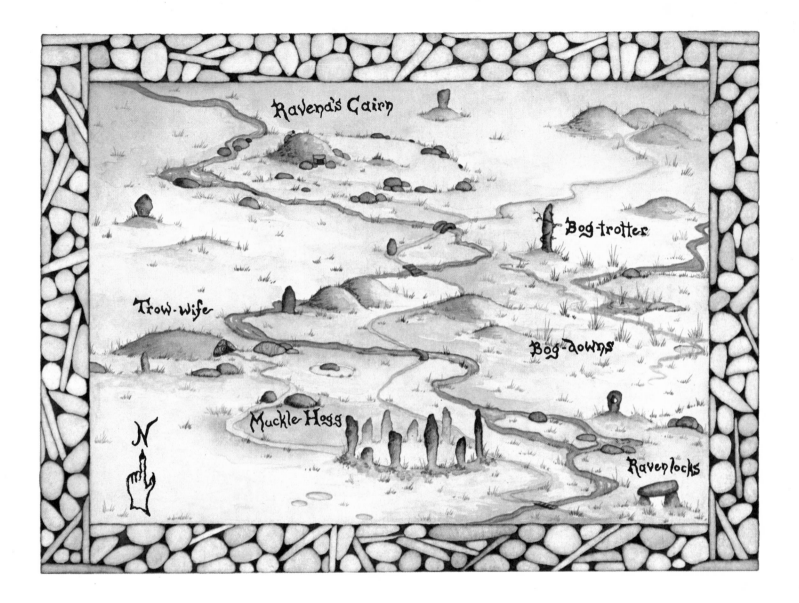

Long ago, deep in the green, stony downs,
lived a small banshee named Ravena.

Ravena belonged to a clan of banshees called the
Ravenlocks. When the Ravenlocks practiced their
wailing, Ravena went off by herself and collected
stones.

When the Ravenlocks met to wash their clothes,
Ravena never helped them. Instead, she disappeared
to gather herbs and tubers for making thin, green
soup.

But what Ravena hated most was when the
Ravenlocks sat by a deep, dark pool, admiring
their craggy faces.

At those times, Ravena stomped
back to her den and scowled
into her spidery mirror. It
cracked each time she looked
into it.

The Ravenlocks screeched with laughter at her cracked mirror. They gagged on her thin, green soup. And they stole her stones and called her Stone-Bones.

Ravena was miserable. And so she decided to leave.
By the light of a sputtering candle, she placed her
favorite stones, her tattered blanket, and her small
iron kettle in her creel. She strapped the creel to
her back and slipped off into the night.

Before starting on her journey, she stopped to say good-bye
to her favorite standing stones, Muckle Hogg.

Then she began walking north.

She walked and walked until she came to a
trow-wife hole. Ravena crawled into the hole,
thinking it would be a safe place to spend the
night.

Suddenly, Ravena bumped into a nose, and it was alive!

"Get out! Get out!" cried a raspy voice. "This is *my* weem. This is not a place for banshees."

Ravena scurried out backwards while the trow-wife poked her with her bony finger.

Once outside, Ravena ran and ran. The ground became
wetter and wetter, and she became more and more
tired. Ravena had come to the bog-downs.

In the distance, she saw a single, standing stone.

She sloshed towards it, hoping to find a place to rest. She slumped down against the stone, out of breath.

From behind the stone, two clammy hands grabbed the little banshee.

"What are you doing in my bogs?" demanded the watery voice of a bog-trotter. "Go away or I'll eat you up!"

Ravena jumped to her feet, leaped across the bogs
before the bog-trotter could eat her, and headed
farther north.

After a while, she came to drier ground. Ravena
was tired and lonely. She rested on top of a
stony mound.

Just as she lay her head on her creel to go to sleep,
she felt the stones move beneath her and—
THUMP—she fell into a dark, damp chamber.
She quickly unpacked her creel and lit a candle.
Stones were everywhere. The entire mound was
built of stones. It was a cairn, and Ravena loved it.

She took her kettle and went outside to fill it with
water. She picked a handful of watercress to make
soup. Then she gathered a few stones and fixed the
hole in the roof.

Ravena made a fire in the fireplace and put her
soup on to cook. She waited for it to boil.

PLOP! Something fell into her kettle.

"What are YOU?" demanded Ravena.

"Elmog," the sooty creature croaked, scrambling out of the kettle. As he fluttered his feathers, Ravena could see that he was a scrawny, old crow.

He flew to a nearby stone and watched hungrily as
Ravena ate her soup.

"Do you want some?" she asked.

"Erghh," said Elmog, flying down and snatching
some watercress out of the kettle.

"Well," asked Ravena, "do you like it?"

"Erp," burped Elmog, as he gobbled it up.

Ravena stretched and yawned.

Then she rolled out her tattered blanket
and crawled into the stony bed.

"Good night, Elmog," she said.

"Erghh," said Elmog, tucking his head
under his wing.

Ravena fell asleep, happy with her new
home and her new friend.